Sky DANCERS

The Amazing World of Canadian Birds

Diane Swanson

Illustrations by Douglas Penhale

Whitecap Books
Vancouver/Toronto

In memory of my dog, Poco,
a pal and constant companion for many years

Whitecap Books
Vancouver/Toronto

Edited by Elaine Jones

Cover design by Kurt Hafso

Interior design by Margaret Ng

Cover and interior illustrations by Douglas Penhale

Typeset by CompuType Graphics, Vancouver, BC

Printed and bound in Canada by D.W. Friesen and Sons Ltd., Altona, Manitoba.

Canadian Cataloguing in Publication Data

Swanson, Diane, 1944–
   Sky dancers

   Includes index.
   ISBN 1-55110-306-0

   1. Birds — Canada — Juvenile literature. 1. Title.
QL685.S92 1995   j598.2971   C95-910305-8

Contents

Here Come the Birds

There are the handsome and the homely. The graceful and the gawky. The heavyweights and the featherweights.

All together, more than 500 different kinds of birds fly Canada's skies. Some live here part time; others, all year round. Some prefer to stay far from people; others nest right in backyards. But wherever birds are, scientists and birdwatchers are gradually learning more about them. And their behaviour is amazing.

Imagine pelicans that turn their pouches inside out. Quails that march up and down mountains. And hummingbirds that beat their wings 5 million times without a rest.

Imagine vultures that ride air bubbles. Starlings that bathe in smoke. And jays that tap windows to be fed.

Birds are so full of surprises it's no wonder we treasure them. And it's no wonder we want to protect them and the places where they live. In Canada, we always want to be able to say: "Here come the birds."

Rufous hummingbird

Hummingbirds
Flying Aces

You can hear them, but they move much too fast to see. The wings of North American hummingbirds beat up to 40 times a second—even faster when the male is courting. They beat so fast they hum. That's how hummingbirds got their name. In fact, the smallest kinds beat their wings faster than any bird on Earth—especially vultures, whose wings beat only once a second.

The family of hummingbirds is huge. It includes about 340 different kinds, all living in North, Central and South America. Four or five kinds nest in the forests, meadows, parks and backyards of Canada.

And as they flit through sunshine, they gleam with greens, reds, purples, oranges and golds. Some of their feathers reflect bright light, creating dazzling colours. Males are the most brilliant; many have especially brightly coloured throats.

Acrobats in Air

No flier can match the hummingbird. It flies forward, backward and side-to-side. Now and then, it flies upside down. It even hovers, holding its place in midair.

The shape of its wings—long, slender and pointed—helps the bird change direction quickly and easily. Unlike other birds' wings, which bend at several joints, hummingbird wings move only at the shoulders. But they swing very freely and in all directions. They can trace figure eights in the air and create power when they beat up as well as down.

Almost from takeoff, hummingbirds fly at full speed. In fact, they start—and stop—faster than most cars. They fly distances as short as a few centimetres, but they also take very long trips each year. Alaska hummingbirds travel 4000 kilometres to Mexico for the winter, then fly back to the same place in Alaska. Hummingbirds heading to Panama from Nova Scotia cross 800 kilometres of water in the Gulf of Mexico with no stops. That's about 5 million wing beats without rest—and the Gulf is just part of the long journey. Some people believe that

Helicopters from Hummingbirds

For centuries, people dreamed about flying machines that could move straight up and down, and whiz this way and that. In the 1890s, a Russian child, named Igor Sikorsky, loved to read about these dreams. He even had some dreams of his own. When he was 12, he built a simple model helicopter that flew. When he was 50—in 1939—he built the world's first full-size, practical helicopter.

To test the new machine, Sikorsky flew it himself. It hovered just above the ground and flew only minutes. But it was a start. "I was sure an aircraft that could fly like a hummingbird would be immensely useful," he said at the time.

In fact, Sikorsky got his best ideas from hummingbirds. He designed his helicopter to take off from a standstill, hover, and fly forward, backward and sideways, just like a hummingbird. By angling their wings—called "blades" on the helicopter—both machine and bird manage to fly well.

hummingbirds hitchhike on other birds, such as Canada geese, but there is no proof for that idea.

Tiny but Tough

Hummingbirds are the world's smallest birds. In Canada—and North America—the tiniest is the calliope hummingbird. No longer than your thumb, it weighs less than a penny. Sometimes people mistake it for a large moth.

As small as hummingbirds are, they are very tough birds. They are especially aggressive when defending their nests and will dive-bomb their enemies, often scaring them off. And compared to hummingbirds, these enemies are giants: chipmunks, cats, snakes, jays, crows, owls, hawks and eagles.

The long, spearlike bill of the hummingbird is not strong enough to use against enemies, but it's good for making threats. And when two hummingbirds fight each other for food, they sometimes use their bills as spears or swords.

Although the normal body temperature for a hummingbird is hotter than yours, the bird is tough enough to live in cold mountain meadows. Its heart helps keep the body warm by beating 1000 times a minute. For its size, the hummingbird has the largest heart of any animal.

To hold heat in, the hummingbird grows a thick feather coat. The ruby-throated hummingbird grows 300 feathers for each gram its body weighs. Like many feather coats, hummingbird coats fill in very early.

Calliope hummingbird

Ruby-throated hummingbird

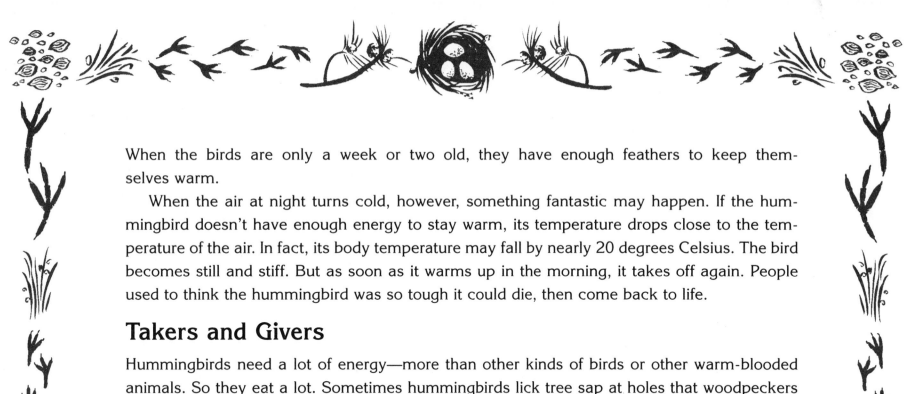

When the birds are only a week or two old, they have enough feathers to keep themselves warm.

When the air at night turns cold, however, something fantastic may happen. If the hummingbird doesn't have enough energy to stay warm, its temperature drops close to the temperature of the air. In fact, its body temperature may fall by nearly 20 degrees Celsius. The bird becomes still and stiff. But as soon as it warms up in the morning, it takes off again. People used to think the hummingbird was so tough it could die, then come back to life.

Takers and Givers

Hummingbirds need a lot of energy—more than other kinds of birds or other warm-blooded animals. So they eat a lot. Sometimes hummingbirds lick tree sap at holes that woodpeckers drill. They also gobble insects, like fruit flies, mosquitoes and small wasps. With their bills open and ready to snap, the birds snatch insects from the air or pluck them from spider webs. They often take the spider webbing, too—to help hold their tiny nests together.

But much of the hummingbird's energy comes from nectar, a sweet liquid in flowers. The bird claims its own feeding territories, sometimes visiting more than 3000 blooms twice a day. It eats most before—and during—its long yearly journeys, often increasing its weight by half. Then it can fly farther between meals.

The hummingbird uses its long, slim bill and its much longer tongue to reach right into blossoms. It does not

Sweet Memories

Hummingbirds have better memories than professors—for some things. In tests at the University of British Columbia, a professor put food into 32 tubes and left 32 other tubes empty. The birds remembered which of all the 64 feeding tubes they could use, even when the professor didn't. They also remembered which tubes held food that was extra sweet.

Hummingbirds have excellent memories for places and patterns in nature as well as in labs. Because they need so much food, it's important that they remember where to find flowers that produce a lot of nectar.

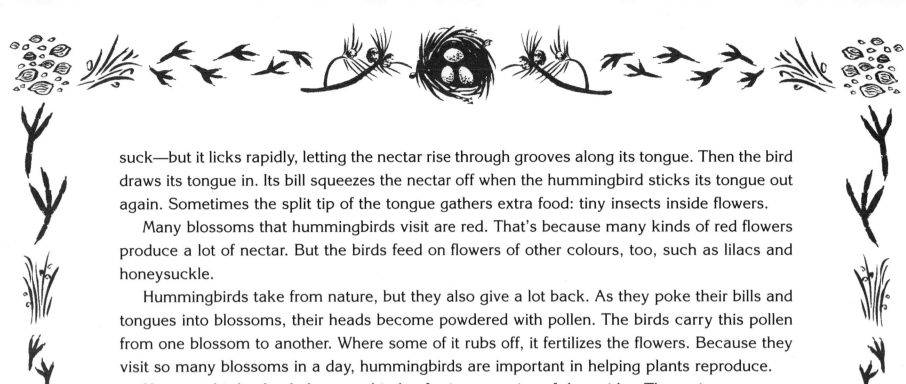

suck—but it licks rapidly, letting the nectar rise through grooves along its tongue. Then the bird draws its tongue in. Its bill squeezes the nectar off when the hummingbird sticks its tongue out again. Sometimes the split tip of the tongue gathers extra food: tiny insects inside flowers.

Many blossoms that hummingbirds visit are red. That's because many kinds of red flowers produce a lot of nectar. But the birds feed on flowers of other colours, too, such as lilacs and honeysuckle.

Hummingbirds take from nature, but they also give a lot back. As they poke their bills and tongues into blossoms, their heads become powdered with pollen. The birds carry this pollen from one blossom to another. Where some of it rubs off, it fertilizes the flowers. Because they visit so many blossoms in a day, hummingbirds are important in helping plants reproduce.

Hummingbirds also help some kinds of mites, cousins of the spider. These tiny creatures live on pollen and nectar in some flowers, but they can't move between blossoms themselves.

Shining Ones with Spears

The Aztec people of Mexico worshipped a mighty war god, named Huitzitzilo-pochtli (say "Hwee-tsee-tsee-lo-potch-tlee"). Once, he had been a brave leader and spear fighter on Earth. But Huitzitzilopochtli had been killed in battle, and his spirit had risen as a hummingbird. *Huitzitzil* means "hummingbird" or "shining one with spear"; *pochtli* means "wizard."

When other Aztec warriors died fighting for their people, they, too, turned into hummingbirds. Together, they formed a noble army led by the hummingbird wizard, Huitzitzilopochtli. Each day, the birds practised spear fighting with their long bills. And each evening, they attacked darkness so it wouldn't forever block out the sun.

So grateful was the sun that it rewarded the hummingbird wizard and his warriors in a very special way. Every time the hummingbirds turned toward the sun, their feathers sparkled—and their throats gleamed like precious rubies and emeralds.

—*an old story from Mexico*

Instead, they hitchhike. As a hummingbird feeds, they run up the bird's bill and into its nostril. Then they dash down when they arrive at the next suitable flower. Mites don't harm either the flowers or the hummingbird.

* * *

Inspecting a bright scarf or deep red lipstick, hummingbirds sometimes check out our world up close. They may even land on someone putting out hummingbird food—or perch on a finger to feed. But some pesticides used in gardens can harm them. If we want these flying aces to return year after year, we must remember to be careful what we put in our yards.

Turkey Vultures
Clean-up Team

As the turkey vulture swoops to the ground, its wings cast a shadow that stretches nearly two metres across. And its big, black-feathered body and long, hooked bill make it look even more threatening. But the vulture doesn't come to kill; its weak bill and claws are not built for attack. Instead, it scavenges food, eating animals that have already died.

Some people call this goose-sized bird a "buzzard." But settlers named it "turkey vulture" because it looks a bit like a turkey. Besides their black bodies, both kinds of birds have small, reddish heads without any feathers.

Turkey vultures live in North and South America. In Canada, they breed in British Columbia, Alberta, Saskatchewan, Manitoba and Ontario. They adapt to many types of land, ranging from deserts to forests.

Scavenger Hunts

Turkey vultures spend a big part of their day flying around in search of food. Using their sharp eyesight, they scan the ground for animals, but they also watch the sky for each other. If one spots food and lands, the others follow. In no time at all, dozens of turkey vultures—some coming from quite a distance—gather at a feeding site.

Few birds are able to smell, but turkey vultures can pick up certain scents. The part of their brain that controls smelling is small compared to many animals but well developed for birds. Vultures use smell as a clue to finding rotten meat in the forest, even when it is under bushes. Still, their keen sight is their most important hunting tool.

The sharp claws of the vulture can rip bits of meat, but its hooked bill is too weak to tear into many kinds of animals. The vulture usually waits for decay to weaken the body or for a stronger scavenger to open it up.

Magnificent *Magnificens*

In Argentina, in 1979, scientists made a stunning discovery. Encased in rock 10 million years old were remains of the largest bird ever to fly on Earth. It weighed 120 kilograms; its wings spanned 7.5 metres—almost as long as four beds placed end-to-end. Until then, no one had ever dreamed a bird could be so big. Scientists named it *Argentavis magnificens.*

This flying dinosaur was closely related to the vultures that live today. But scientists don't think it was a scavenger. Instead, they believe it was a fierce predator able to compete with mammals for food.

Then the turkey vulture uses its rough tongue like a file to scrape meat from the bones. And it can push its featherless head right into a body without any of the meat clinging to it. Although dead bodies often contain dangerous germs, vultures feed safely. Without harming itself, a single vulture can take in more germs than would be needed to kill a buffalo.

Unlike some other birds, turkey vultures can't use their bills or feet to carry food to their nests. Their feet can't even close. Instead, vultures

swallow all the food they can, and then vomit it up for their young in ground nests or hollow logs.

Being able to vomit at will also helps protect the vulture. The strong smell usually drives animals away. Even young vultures in the nest throw up their food if a skunk or raccoon threatens them. Sometimes they will even vomit right on their enemy.

Bubble Rides

It's morning and the turkey vulture waits—waits for the sun to warm the ground and the ground to warm the air. The warm air forms a big bubble on the ground. There it grows until it breaks free and rises. Called a

One of the Gang

Birds don't have thermals all to themselves. Pilots of motorless planes, called gliders, also ride these warm air bubbles. After airplanes tow them high into the air, glider pilots depend on thermals to stay airborne. Like turkey vultures, they spiral upward inside thermals, then glide down and fly up again in other thermals.

Glider pilots have flown with turkey vultures, sharing the same thermal at the same time. Sometimes the birds react by keeping a close watch on the glider. But they soon seem to accept it as something that belongs in the sky. The pilot becomes one of the gang and they all fly gracefully together.

thermal, the bubble rises higher and higher, and a billowy cloud forms on top of it.

Turkey vultures fly in thermals, spiralling upward inside them. When they reach the top, the birds glide gradually down to the bottom of the next thermal. Flying and gliding, flying and gliding, they move from thermal to thermal. They may rise 2000 metres in one and glide for several kilometres before they reach the next thermal.

By riding bubbles, turkey vultures fly high and far without using much energy. That makes it easier for them to search large areas for food, which is often widely scattered.

The wings of the vulture are well designed for soaring. They are long and broad to catch the air. They have fingerlike feathers that spread to help the bird turn circles inside thermals. And if gusts of wind tip the bird, it levels itself by twisting one wing tip down and the other up. This twisting gave American Wilbur Wright—a pioneer in developing airplanes—a great idea. He designed gliders with wings that pilots could twist.

Frozen Stiff

When ice statues blink, you know they're more than ice. That's what one boy decided when he spotted several frozen turkey vultures standing on snow. They had spent the night in freezing rain. By morning, their backs and wings had become coated with ice and they had fallen stiffly from the trees.

With help from his family, the boy gently removed ice from the feathers until a few of the birds were able to fly. But the others stood with their wings frozen by their sides.

The family put these vultures in a barn overnight. In the morning, the birds walked out into warm sunshine and soon were able to fly again.

Soaring for long periods can bend a turkey vulture's flight feathers. But the cure is easy. With wings outspread, the bird perches in the sun until its feathers straighten out. That takes only about five minutes, but if the vulture is stuck in shade, it can take three hours.

Mating Games

The turkey vulture sings no love song. It has no voice box so it makes few sounds. When the male goes courting, he groans—a soft, low groan—and inflates air sacs in his neck. He raises his wings high

but keeps them folded. Then he rocks side to side, raising his feet one at a time. On he goes, dragging his tail and slowly moving forward. When he stops, he may click his bill a few times.

The male also does a dance with his partner. It's a lively dance. The two birds face each other, bills hanging open. They spread their wings wide and move up and down fast. First one, then the other jumps in the air. "Yap, yap, yap," they call. Then one bird lowers its head, placing its bill on the ground.

Most turkey vultures save all their dances for their mates. They stay partners for life.

*　　*　　*

It's a good thing there are turkey vultures. On the ground, they are nature's clean-up team, feeding on dead animals and recycling decaying flesh. In the air, they put on a first-class air show, soaring high in the sky, then gliding majestically down again.

Steller's jay

Jays

Big Talkers

The feathers on some jays' heads can "talk." Standing up on end they say: "I'm ready to fight." The straighter they stand, the tougher they talk. These feathers, called a crest, can also stand on end when the birds are excited. But when jays rest or feed calmly, the crest usually lies flat.

Jays live in many countries; blue, Steller's and gray jays live in Canada. Both blue and Steller's jays talk with their crests. And both look mostly blue, but their colour is a trick. Like soap bubbles, their feathers bend and reflect light, creating colour. Crush a feather and the blue disappears.

The gray jay, or Canada jay, is different. It has no crest and its colour is grey—just as its name says. It lives across Canada, while Steller's jays live mostly west of the Rocky Mountains and blue jays live mostly east. All three kinds of jays stay in Canada year round, but some blue jays move south for the winter.

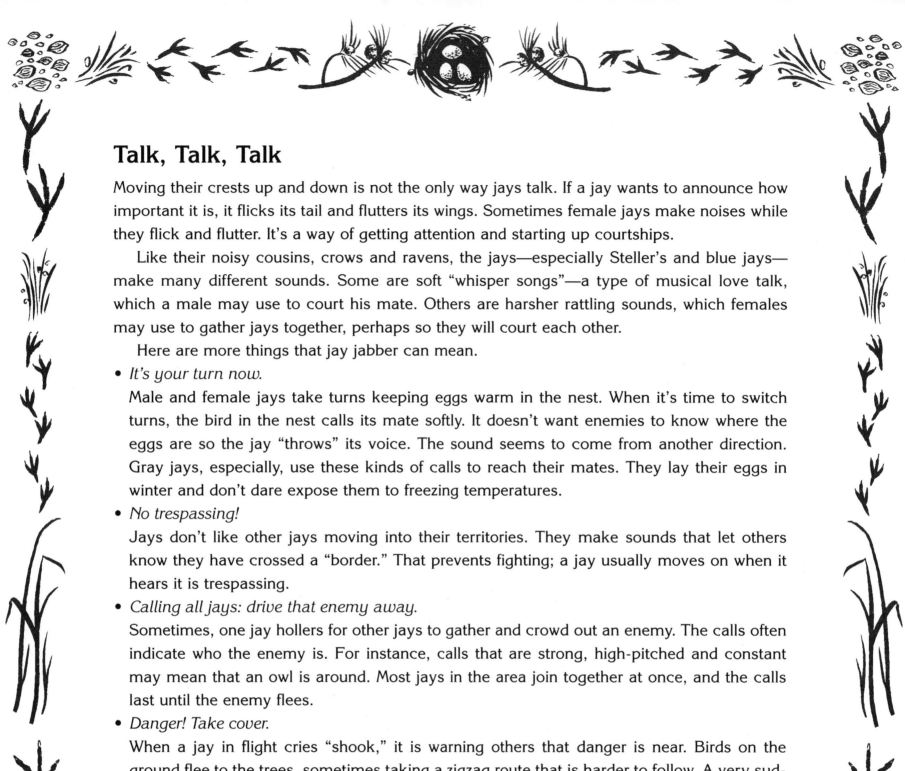

Talk, Talk, Talk

Moving their crests up and down is not the only way jays talk. If a jay wants to announce how important it is, it flicks its tail and flutters its wings. Sometimes female jays make noises while they flick and flutter. It's a way of getting attention and starting up courtships.

Like their noisy cousins, crows and ravens, the jays—especially Steller's and blue jays—make many different sounds. Some are soft "whisper songs"—a type of musical love talk, which a male may use to court his mate. Others are harsher rattling sounds, which females may use to gather jays together, perhaps so they will court each other.

Here are more things that jay jabber can mean.

- *It's your turn now.*
Male and female jays take turns keeping eggs warm in the nest. When it's time to switch turns, the bird in the nest calls its mate softly. It doesn't want enemies to know where the eggs are so the jay "throws" its voice. The sound seems to come from another direction. Gray jays, especially, use these kinds of calls to reach their mates. They lay their eggs in winter and don't dare expose them to freezing temperatures.

- *No trespassing!*
Jays don't like other jays moving into their territories. They make sounds that let others know they have crossed a "border." That prevents fighting; a jay usually moves on when it hears it is trespassing.

- *Calling all jays: drive that enemy away.*
Sometimes, one jay hollers for other jays to gather and crowd out an enemy. The calls often indicate who the enemy is. For instance, calls that are strong, high-pitched and constant may mean that an owl is around. Most jays in the area join together at once, and the calls last until the enemy flees.

- *Danger! Take cover.*
When a jay in flight cries "shook," it is warning others that danger is near. Birds on the ground flee to the trees, sometimes taking a zigzag route that is harder to follow. A very sudden, harsh "shook" may warn others of a particular danger—a hawk.

Grab and Stash

Jays eat a lot and they eat many different kinds of food, including fruits, nuts, grains, insects, frogs and small snakes. They also eat camp food, like bacon and biscuits, and pet food, like kibbles for dogs. Some eat garbage and nonfood, such as bits of hand soap.

Jays also steal eggs and young birds from nests. They may imitate a hawk's cry to scare parent birds away from the nests. But some parent birds play their own tricks to protect their young from jays. For instance, birds called flycatchers may weave a cast-off snakeskin into the edge of their nest. Part of the skin dangles down and scares the jays away.

In cities, jays often lunch at birdfeeders—especially if they spot sunflower seeds and peanuts. These birds tend to be greedy eaters. A blue or Steller's jay can hold five peanuts in its bill at the same time.

But even jays can't eat all the food they find. They store some in cracks or hollows in trees. They hide some on the ground under leaves and grass. They press some into snow. Around houses, jays may also hammer nuts into a lawn, garden bed or flower box. One was seen covering a buried peanut with a rock twice as big as its head. The bird dragged and pushed the rock until it rolled on top of

Time to Be Quiet

As noisy as jays are, they know when it's best to say nothing at all. In one small town, a pair of blue jays built their nest in a tree very near the entrance of a store. The female laid her eggs and the pair took turns caring for them.

Customers came and customers went, but they didn't know the jays were there. They didn't hear them and they didn't see them. When either of the birds approached the nest, it stopped first in a shrub close to the tree. Then it crept quietly to the branches of the tree and sneaked its way to the nest.

Once, when the female was in the nest, she noticed someone looking her way. She flattened herself against her eggs and she didn't make a sound. You could scarcely tell she was there.

Gray jay

the peanut. Jays seem to remember many of their hiding places and return later to feed—especially during winter.

Gray jays have a special way of banking meals. They use their tongues to roll food into small balls, which they coat with sticky saliva. Then they stash these balls in a tree hollow or among the needles of evergreen branches.

Food balls not only help adult gray jays live through winter, they are important food for young jays. The hardy gray jay nests as early as February, when the snow makes other food hard to find.

Act Up, Settle Down

A jay is smaller than a crow, but it teases bigger animals, such as hawks, owls and, sometimes, cats. One jay swooped down near a curled-up cat asleep on a sunny step. It hopped closer and closer until it took a quick peck at the cat's tail. Then—swoosh—it charged off, just beyond the cat's reach.

Like cats, jays lie in the sunlight and bathe in the heat. They spread out their wings and tails, lifting their feathers to let the sunlight in. It just seems to feel good.

Something else that must feel good is called "anting." Crouching over ants on the ground, the jay spreads out its wings. Sometimes it turns its tail sideways to the earth. Then it lets ants crawl all over its body.

The bird also picks up ants with its bill and places them on its feathers. Reaching

Happy Campers

In forests and alpine meadows, the gray jay often visits campsites where it earns its nickname: camp robber. Not only does it hop about, picking crumbs off the ground, it steals from sandwiches on unguarded plates. Eager jays even snatch pieces of pancake from the forks of startled campers.

Most people enjoy jays at camps and along hiking trails. The birds are often brave enough to feed out of hand. Even without trying, a snacking hiker can attract a gray jay. One loud crunch on a cracker can draw a jay out of nowhere to land on a knee or a wrist.

Blue jay

around to put ants under its wings, a jay can become so excited that it trips over its own tail.

Anting seems to be a mystery. Some people think that a liquid from ants may help kill lice on the bird. Others think that the liquid works like oil to help the jay care for its feathers. But no one knows for sure—except the jay.

* * *

Some people like blue jays because they feed their young hundreds of tent caterpillars, which harm fruit trees. But whether or not jays help save trees, they're playful, chatty birds. Our backyards and forests wouldn't be as much fun without them.

Knock, Knock. Who's There?

It happens. People hear a knock, answer the door and find no one there. Sometimes it is a person playing a joke, but other times it is a jay.

Jays bang seeds and nuts to open them. When they do it on the roof, it can sound like someone knocking on the door. The noise often fools people.

But some jays really do knock. A woman who feeds jays in her yard said one tapped on her window to remind her that it was time. The bird kept tapping until she put out the food.

Other jays are less pushy. Some just hang upside down from the roof gutter, staring through the window until they're noticed—and fed.

Cooper's hawk

Forest Hawks
Agile Hunters

When one animal hunts another, there's often a race—a fast-paced race. Nothing odd about that, except when the race takes place in a forest. Imagine a bird so skilled it can fly full speed through a maze of tree trunks—even plunging through thick brush to catch its quarry. Imagine a forest hawk, one of the most agile hunters of all.

Three kinds of forest hawks live in Canada. They nest all across the nation and in several other countries around the world. The northern goshawk is the largest—about 60 centimetres long. The smallest, the sharp-shinned hawk, is about half that. In between is the Cooper's hawk, which is close to the size of a crow.

The hawks look a lot alike, all blue-grey on top. Beneath, the two smaller hawks are reddish-brown and the northern goshawk is light grey.

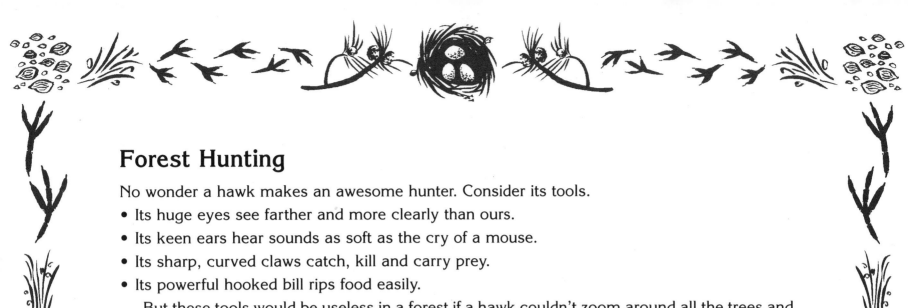

Forest Hunting

No wonder a hawk makes an awesome hunter. Consider its tools.

- Its huge eyes see farther and more clearly than ours.
- Its keen ears hear sounds as soft as the cry of a mouse.
- Its sharp, curved claws catch, kill and carry prey.
- Its powerful hooked bill rips food easily.

But these tools would be useless in a forest if a hawk couldn't zoom around all the trees and bushes. That's where the design of its wings and tail comes in. Rounded wings help the hawk make great bursts of speed. And like a rudder, its long tail helps the hawk make sharp, sudden turns. With rapid wingbeats and short glides, it speeds through the forest, dodging tree trunks and branches deftly as it goes.

Forest hawks mostly hunt alone, but they have several hunting styles. Still and silent, a hawk—especially a Cooper's hawk—may perch on a branch until it spots prey. Then it shoots down like a bullet. It brakes hard with its tail, stretches out its claws and grabs.

Sometimes a northern goshawk cruises until it spots a meal. When it's about nine metres to touchdown, it glides, low and fast. Then, two metres to target, it hurls its feet forward and strikes. A Cooper's or a sharp-shinned hawk may use surprise as a weapon. It bursts through woods, startling small prey out of hiding and taking after them. It may scatter a flock of small birds and then focus the chase on just one.

Once a hawk has captured a bird, it usually takes the prey to a plucking post where it pulls out the feathers.

Catching a Bite to Eat

When two hawks unite to form a pair, the male brings gifts. He catches prey and presents them to his mate. Sometimes, he serves her as she perches in a tree. At other times, she flies out to meet him. Like pilots in an aerial acrobatic team, the hawks zoom toward each other. As they draw close, the male flies just a bit higher than the female. Then, with split-second timing, he drops the food, and she grabs it with her feet.

Northern goshawk

Hawks in Hand

For many centuries and in many countries, people enjoyed hawking, or falconry. They trained hawks to hunt small animals, like game birds and rabbits. The Chinese even trained small hawks to hunt butterflies. Sometimes people used dogs to scare prey out of bushes. As the prey took off, hawks chased it down.

In Europe during the Middle Ages (500 A.D. to about 1500), many rich and royal people kept trained northern goshawks. They carried the birds perched on their wrists all day. At meal times, the hawks sat behind their owners. Even religious leaders, like bishops and abbots, liked to keep their birds with them. They took the hawks into churches and monasteries, keeping them on altar railings during services.

The post may be a large level bough, stump or old nest. All forest hawks eat birds and some rodents. Northern goshawks also eat other animals, like rabbits, squirrels and snakes.

Sky Dancing

When spring comes to the forest, it's time to dance. Hawks—especially northern goshawks—take to the skies with a message: "This area is mine." They also dance to bond with their mates. It's usually the female that dances, but the male joins her at times. Calling to one another or flying in silence, they perform their art in the morning air.

They move like waves as they rise up and glide down. Wave follows wave across the wide sky. Then they circle up high, slowly flapping their wings, and they make more waves that slope gradually down. Sometimes the dancers plunge suddenly to the trees or shoot upward and circle sky-high again.

Occasionally, the male takes the lead. Soaring briefly in the sky, he dives toward the female. Or he may chase her beneath the treetops where they fly slowly, beating their wings, then gliding—beating, then gliding.

Hawks in Focus

It's tough—and very dangerous—to take pictures of forest hawks in their nests. It means spending days up a tree, getting cold, damp and cramped, and nights in a forest, sleeping without a fire.

Professional photographers try hard not to attract attention. They usually build small blinds—enclosures to hide in—right up in the trees. They build these blinds bit by bit so the hawks get used to them. Then the photographers climb into their blinds before sunrise each day, always wearing clothes of the same colour.

Despite all this care, photographers still risk serious attacks from hawks protecting their nests. Sometimes the birds buzz them again and again. Then it's time to drop to the bottom of the blind and wait until the hawks settle down again.

Home Making

When it's time to lay eggs, it's time to make a home. A pair of hawks may fix up an old nest or build a new one. Hawks prefer a nest in a tree that is close to water and a plucking post. And they always prefer a home that is well hidden, often near the trunk of a large tree. It's not easy to spot the nest of a forest hawk.

The smallest hawks have the biggest families. Sharp-shinned hawks raise up to eight young, so they build broad nests. Cooper's hawks have smaller nests and raise up to five young. They prefer to build or repair their homes in a three-way fork of a large tree branch.

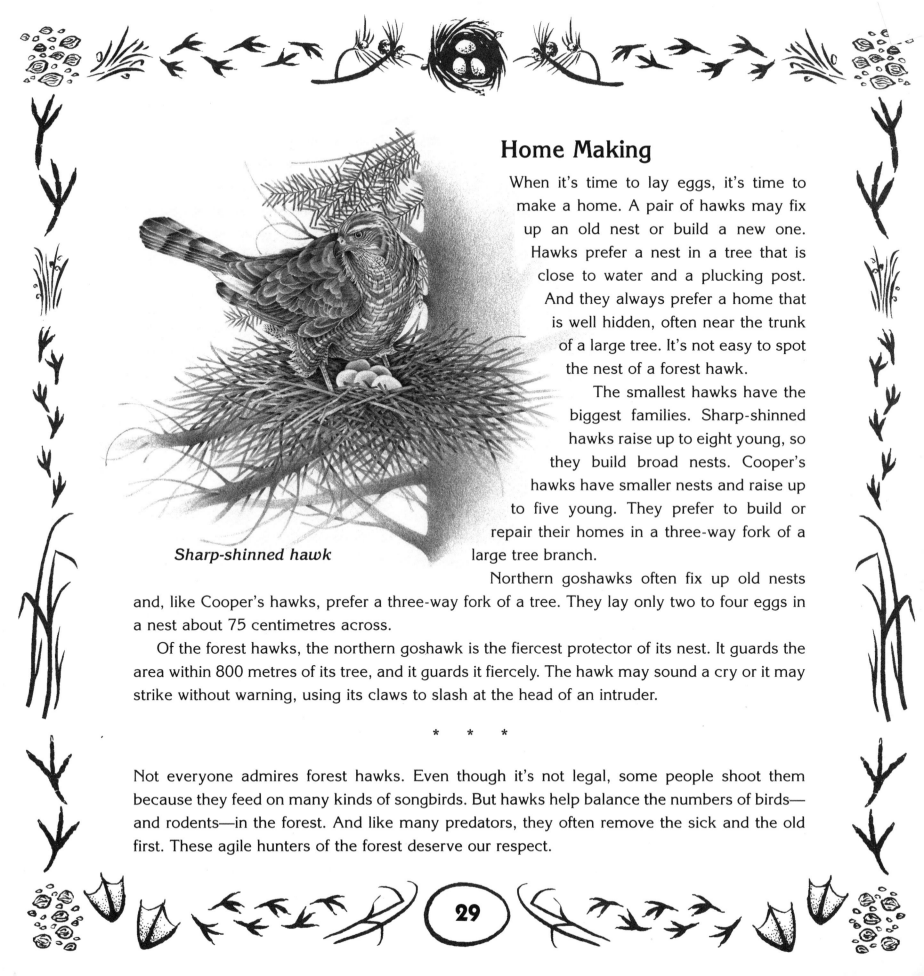

Sharp-shinned hawk

Northern goshawks often fix up old nests and, like Cooper's hawks, prefer a three-way fork of a tree. They lay only two to four eggs in a nest about 75 centimetres across.

Of the forest hawks, the northern goshawk is the fiercest protector of its nest. It guards the area within 800 metres of its tree, and it guards it fiercely. The hawk may sound a cry or it may strike without warning, using its claws to slash at the head of an intruder.

*　　*　　*

Not everyone admires forest hawks. Even though it's not legal, some people shoot them because they feed on many kinds of songbirds. But hawks help balance the numbers of birds—and rodents—in the forest. And like many predators, they often remove the sick and the old first. These agile hunters of the forest deserve our respect.

Tufted puffin

Puffins
Change Artists

Many animals change from season to season. They put on a thicker coat or even turn a different colour. But when it comes to making big changes, there's nothin' like a puffin. It adopts a whole new look before it breeds—changing colours and growing bill and eye ornaments. It looks so different during nesting seasons that people once thought Canada had six kinds of puffins instead of three.

The Atlantic puffin—also called the common puffin—breeds along Atlantic coasts of North America and Europe. More than six out of every ten of the North American birds nest on small islands in Witless Bay, Newfoundland. The horned puffin, which sometimes sports dark, fleshy "horns" above its eyes, breeds along Pacific coasts of North America and on islands in the Bering Sea. The tufted puffin, named for the hairlike tufts of feathers on its head when it nests, breeds in the same general area as the horned puffin.

Dressing and Undressing

Each spring, just before breeding, puffins "dress" for courting. Ornaments, like rings and horns, appear around their eyes. Their legs and feet turn bright orange or red. New, black feathers replace old feathers on their backs, while their faces become mostly white. And long clusters of corn-coloured feathers grow down from the heads of tufted puffins and curl onto their shoulders.

But the most dramatic changes happen to the puffins' bills: they grow larger and take on brilliant colours. The Atlantic puffin gains a bill that is striped orange-red and blue with thick, yellow markings. The bill of the horned puffin turns a radiant yellow with a deep red tip. The tufted puffin develops an orange-red bill with a greenish base on the upper part.

After the nesting season, however, puffins lose their courting outfits. They shed their eye ornaments. Legs and feet fade to pale yellow. Dull brownish feathers appear on their backs, and their white faces become grey. The tufted puffin sheds its quirky yellow head feathers, and the covering on its bill falls off in seven brightly coloured pieces. The Atlantic puffin loses the outer layers of its bill in nine pieces. After they leave their nesting colonies, the bills of all three puffins are reduced to drab little beaks, no more than two-thirds their former size.

The Name Game

Clowns of the sea. That's what puffins are called. And it's easy to understand why. They are plump with large heads, stubby tails, short legs and wide feet. When they walk, they waddle. But it's their colourful, oversized bills that make these seabirds look really clownlike at breeding time.

The puffin's big, bright bill is the reason the bird has several other names, too. Some people call the Atlantic puffin sea parrot, bottlenose, goldenhead, or even just plain "Bill." But when they talk about the tufted puffin, they often use a different name: old man of the sea. The long feathers on the bird's head at breeding times make it look like an aging fellow.

Milling and Billing

When it's time to breed, puffins gather in colonies on sea coasts, usually on islands, where they have fewer enemies, such as rats. They mill about on slopes near the water, preparing their nests. Often they return to the same nests they used the year before—first cleaning them out.

Most nest in ground burrows or among rocks. Where it's hard to dig, they move into burrows made by other animals, like rabbits. But often they dig their own burrows. Using their heavy bills and strong claws, puffins chisel the ground. Then they shovel out the soil with their webbed feet. They don't fuss much with a lining, but they usually scatter grass, seaweed and a few feathers in their burrows.

Puffins often pair for life. And during breeding seasons, the pairs bond through activities such as "billing." Swinging its bill, a puffin walks toward its partner. Then one bird may nibble the other bird. Next the two bang their thick bills noisily together—again and again. As they clash, one of the birds often raises the feathers of its neck and head. The other bird presses its feathers flat. And they both tilt their tails and step slowly round and round on the spot.

Bird, Fish or King?

For more than 1000 years, people in Europe believed there were animals that were part bird and part fish or shellfish. "Bird-fish," they thought, began life in the sea, then took on the shape of birds. One of the first bird-fish was a goose that formed inside goose barnacles on floating wood at sea.

Later, the Atlantic puffin became the bird-fish of England and Wales. Although it looked like a bird, people believed it was mainly a fish. They ate a lot of puffins when their religion would not allow them to eat anything but fish.

But to some people in parts of Britain, the puffin was neither bird nor fish. It was the spirit of their King Arthur, who took the form of the seabird to visit his favourite spots.

Atlantic puffin

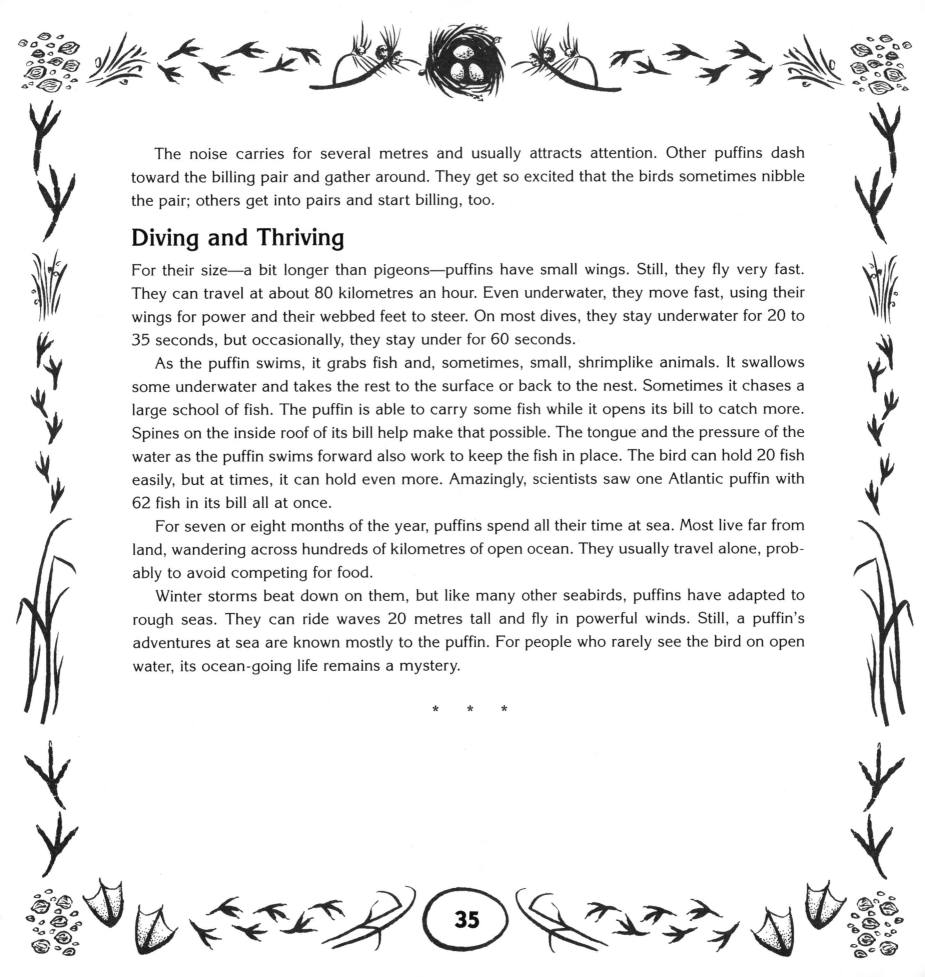

The noise carries for several metres and usually attracts attention. Other puffins dash toward the billing pair and gather around. They get so excited that the birds sometimes nibble the pair; others get into pairs and start billing, too.

Diving and Thriving

For their size—a bit longer than pigeons—puffins have small wings. Still, they fly very fast. They can travel at about 80 kilometres an hour. Even underwater, they move fast, using their wings for power and their webbed feet to steer. On most dives, they stay underwater for 20 to 35 seconds, but occasionally, they stay under for 60 seconds.

As the puffin swims, it grabs fish and, sometimes, small, shrimplike animals. It swallows some underwater and takes the rest to the surface or back to the nest. Sometimes it chases a large school of fish. The puffin is able to carry some fish while it opens its bill to catch more. Spines on the inside roof of its bill help make that possible. The tongue and the pressure of the water as the puffin swims forward also work to keep the fish in place. The bird can hold 20 fish easily, but at times, it can hold even more. Amazingly, scientists saw one Atlantic puffin with 62 fish in its bill all at once.

For seven or eight months of the year, puffins spend all their time at sea. Most live far from land, wandering across hundreds of kilometres of open ocean. They usually travel alone, probably to avoid competing for food.

Winter storms beat down on them, but like many other seabirds, puffins have adapted to rough seas. They can ride waves 20 metres tall and fly in powerful winds. Still, a puffin's adventures at sea are known mostly to the puffin. For people who rarely see the bird on open water, its ocean-going life remains a mystery.

*   *   *

Horned puffin

Puffins have been having a tough time—mostly because of people, who have overhunted them. The birds have also died from tangling in fishing gear, eating bits of plastic and getting soaked in oil. On some islands, animals such as rats, cats, dogs, raccoons and foxes—many brought in by people—have attacked puffin nests. Commercial fishing has reduced the puffins' food, and tourists have disturbed their nesting.

But people are working to protect puffins more and create a healthier ocean for all. They want to keep these charming change artists coming to Canada's coasts.

Salty Seabird

Puffins take in a lot of salty sea water. They gulp it down while grabbing fish and other food in the ocean. They also drink from the sea. It's normally their only source of water during the non-breeding season.

Most animals can't drink sea water because of all the salt it contains. But the puffin, like other seabirds, has special glands in the front of its head that help get rid of the extra salt. These glands draw salt from the bird into a liquid that runs out the nostrils in the bill. Puffins are able to get rid of more salt than any other seabird.

Mountain quail

Quails

Close Clan

In the bushes there's a swish—a blended rustling of 24 tiny feet through dry grass. A dozen quail chicks are rushing to line up, single file, behind one parent while the other parent looks on. This is a family that takes family living seriously. Long after the birds leave the nest, they stick together, finding food and facing danger as a group.

Quails are small birds—up to 28 centimetres tall. They can fly, but they spend most of their time on the ground. Their feet are well built for walking and running.

Related to turkeys, pheasants, partridges and grouse, quails live around the globe. In Canada, however, they are an oddity—and very special. There's the California quail in the lowlands of southwestern British Columbia. The brown female and blue-grey male each wears six black feathers curved in a floppy, comma-shaped plume on its head. And although it's very rare in Canada, there's

Northern bobwhite

the chestnut-coloured mountain quail in the highlands of southwestern British Columbia. It sports a long, straight plume of two black feathers.

A quail with no plume at all lives in southern Ontario fields. The brown-and-white northern bobwhite gets its name from its clear "bob-white" call. During spring and summer, it's the common cry of unmated males announcing: "I'm here."

All in the Family

Quails build simple nests—hollows in the ground—which they dig with their toes and claws. The birds line the nests with grass and bits of leaves. Shrubs hide most nests, but northern bobwhites weave a grassy arch over theirs.

Depending on the kind of quail, females lay up to 18 eggs. The males help care for them. Usually both parent birds take turns keeping the eggs warm for about three weeks. If one quail dies, the other cares for the eggs alone. Sometimes a female lays a second set of eggs and leaves her mate to care for the first set.

The parent birds protect their eggs and chicks from attacks by enemies such as hawks, snakes, raccoons, cats and dogs. Each year, however, a number of chicks are killed. That's one reason quails have such large families.

Quail chicks leave the nest the same day they hatch. As soon as their feathers are dry, they take off after their

Quail Math-EGG-matics

What great egg-makers quails are. They can channel much of the energy they get from food into egg production. A single batch of bobwhite or California quail eggs weighs about 90 per cent as much as the female who lays them. That is, a quail weighing 167 grams may lay 14 eggs weighing 11 grams each—a total of 154 grams. By comparison, a woman who weighs 55 kilograms may give birth to a baby who weighs 3.5 kilograms— only about 6 per cent of her weight.

The fact that quails often lay eggs more than once a year makes their egg-producing ability especially amazing. Some quails have been known to lay over 100 eggs in a year.

parents, running around and looking for food. Still, the parent birds use their wings to warm the chicks for another two weeks—until the feathers on the young birds fill in.

Each kind of quail speaks its own language. The birds use calls, whistles and songs to talk to each other. Bobwhites make the greatest number of sounds—24. They call "hoypoo" or "hoy," for instance, if they are separated from their mates. And they repeat "tu-tu" to announce, "Hey, there's some great food over here."

California quails use about 14 different calls, including "ut, ut" notes to help stay together. The males make high-pitched whistles to threaten other males during breeding seasons. Mountain quails rally together with a loud "cle-cle-cle" or "kow-kow-kow," but sound an alarm with a shrill "t-t-t-r-r-r-r-rt."

Fortunetelling Quails

Unlike quails in North America, quails in Europe travel quite far each spring and fall. Europeans once tried to tell their fortunes by listening to the calls of quails as they came and went with the seasons. In Austria, for instance, young people counted the calls of the first quail they heard each spring. That number told them how many years would pass before they got married.

As summer ended, peasants in countries such as Germany, Italy, France and Switzerland listened carefully to the quail. They believed the bird's calls indicated how much money they would get for their corn in the fall. For example, three calls from a quail in the corn field meant that the crop would sell for three coins a basket.

Safety in Numbers

Except when they are nesting, quails live in a covey—a group of relatives plus a few others. Mountain quails usually form the smallest coveys, of about 9 birds each. Northern bobwhites often gather in groups of 14 and sometimes merge with other coveys to form large flocks. But a covey of California quails is the biggest of all—about 40 to 60 birds—and the quails sometimes band together in groups as big as 200.

Quails in a covey get along well. They help each other find food, keep warm and stay safe. When they rest, they

often snuggle side by side in a circle, tails pointing in and heads pointing out. They raise their wings slightly, forming an unbroken cover that helps keep their body heat in. Then they listen and watch—all around the circle—for signs of danger. If any of them senses a threat, the covey bursts apart. Each bird zooms off in its own direction, flustering the enemy.

Sometimes male quails in a covey take turns as lookouts while the others eat or sleep. If there's trouble, they sound the alarm by crying out. It may be a general alarm or one that warns of an enemy on the ground or in the air.

When something threatens their eggs, parent birds may cry and pretend they are hurt by dragging their wings. That often draws enemies to the parent—and away from the nest. Then the parent can take off and sneak back to the nest when danger has passed.

At the sound of an alarm, adult quails can run and fly fast to escape, but very young chicks cannot. Instead they often crouch, freezing on the spot. The colour of their feathers blends with the grass and dirt so well that quail chicks are very hard to spot.

Hanging around Home

Quails, especially northern bobwhites, are stay-at-home birds. Most live their whole life within several kilometres of where they hatched.

The most mobile is the mountain quail. During the nesting season and through summer, it lives quite high on hills and mountains. The weather is generally cooler there—sometimes too cool for the quails to stay year round. So in the fall, the mountain quail heads downslope to spend the winter in warmer grounds.

Rub-a-Dub-Dust

Where there's little water but plenty of dirt, some animals bathe in dust. Using the claws on their feet, quails scratch up the ground. They ruffle their feathers and work their heads and wings right into the dirt. Once they are covered with dust, they shake it all off again.

One person who watched the same northern bobwhite all summer noticed it always shook three times—never more and never less—after taking each dust bath.

California quail

Travelling together in small groups, mountain quails walk single file down the slope. They move along leisurely, rarely flying, except to cross things like gullies or ditches. When spring comes, they head back up again, walking most of the way.

When quails need to eat and drink, they don't have to go far from home. California quails mostly feed on leaves and seeds in the bushy areas around them. They also eat some grains and fruits, and just a few insects. If there is no water to drink, they survive by feeding on juicy plants.

Mountain quails also eat leaves and seeds as well as other plant parts, like buds and roots. They can even peel and eat an unripened acorn, opening the shell at its soft, green base. And over the summer, they eat a few insects. Unlike California quails, mountain quails need to drink water, so they make sure that home is close to a stream or pond.

Northern bobwhites eat the greatest variety of food—all found nearby. They eat mostly plants, but they also feed on snails, daddy longlegs, inchworms, ants, flies, mosquitoes and bees. Some moisture comes from juicy food, but the quails also need to drink water. Early in the morning, they often lick the dew off blades of grass.

*　　*　　*

For some people, the best sights and sounds of spring come from quails: a long string of chicks scurrying through the grass with their parents. Although hunters shoot quails, people who spray crops and build houses in quail territory harm a greater number. Let's hope we always leave room in Canada for the quail—and its very close clan.

Pileated woodpecker

Woodpeckers
Distant Drummers

From the forest comes a drum roll. Then another and another. Each one begins slowly and softly, grows fast and loud, then fades away. From inside a house more than two kilometres away, you can hear the loudest beats.

The drummer is Canada's largest woodpecker, beating its bill on a hollow branch, high in a big, old tree. The crow-sized bird, called the pileated (say "pie-lee-ated") woodpecker, beats on a hard, bare spot turned white from steady use. It beats, then listens to the echo—or, sometimes, to another woodpecker drumming back. Then it beats again, shaking its whole black-and-white body and the bright red feathers on its head.

About 200 kinds of woodpeckers live around the world; 14 in Canada. The downy woodpecker (Canada's smallest woodpecker), the hairy woodpecker, the yellow-bellied sapsucker and the northern flicker are some of the other kinds of woodpeckers that live in every province and both territories of the country.

Hammer Heads

A big part of being a woodpecker is pecking wood. Many woodpeckers peck trees to make homes for themselves and to find food, like insects. They peck to send messages that attract mates or claim territory. For that, they choose "signal posts"—trees or metal objects, like drain spouts—that sound especially loud when pecked. Some kinds of woodpeckers also "knock" softly before they enter their tree homes.

The woodpecker is well designed to peck wood. It has a tough, chisel-like bill and a head that can stand the shock of all that hammering. Its skull is thick and heavy, and cushions of air cradle its brain. Stiff tail feathers support the bird while huge neck muscles work the head like a hammer. Strong legs and feet hold the woodpecker's body in place. Its claws—sharp and curving—grip the trees. On most woodpeckers, one toe and claw can bend sideways to strengthen the grip.

The Unwilling Woodpecker

When Earth was new, birds everywhere began to dig hollows in the ground with their bills. The hollows would fill with water, forming the planet's rivers and lakes. All the birds helped—except the unwilling woodpecker. It simply refused to dig.

After the work was done, the other birds told the woodpecker, "Because you refused to peck the ground, you must forever peck wood. Because you refused to help make the rivers and lakes, you must forever drink only rain."

To this day, woodpeckers peck wood and cling upright to trees, as though ready to catch raindrops.

—*an old story from Europe*

Tricky Tongues

Although most woodpeckers eat some plant food, like berries, they mostly feed on young insects. Favourites include termites, carpenter ants and beetles that live and feed in trees. The birds claim big territories as their hunting grounds. One pileated woodpecker alone may claim as many as 80 hectares.

The woodpecker hunts for insects just beneath the bark or well inside the trees. It has excellent sight to search for signs of insects and keen hearing to listen for their munching. When it finds the right spot, it drills a hole, flinging away bark and wood. Then it shoves its tongue inside.

Twice as long as the head of most woodpeckers, the tongue is a marvel. It's skinny and it's sticky. It has a great sense of touch, and its tip is armed with sharp, backward-pointing spines. Pushing its tongue into the tree well beyond the end of its bill, the woodpecker feels about for insects. Then it stabs them with the spines on its tongue and draws them out. A sticky coating on the tongue makes sure the insects don't rub off along the way.

Power Poles Meet Woodpecker Power

To woodpeckers, a tree and a wooden pole are much the same. And that can cause problems for workers who check power lines carrying electricity from pole to pole—and city to city.

Although the birds mostly drill wood containing insects, they sometimes search new, insect-free poles for food. Some experts think that woodpeckers mistake the humming of power lines for the buzzing or munching of insects.

Power line workers have even reported woodpeckers attacking poles while they were still being raised. The birds seemed to be testing the sound of the wood. Or perhaps they wanted to carve out a home. Pileated woodpeckers have drilled nesting holes 60 centimetres deep and 15 centimetres wide in new power poles. When one worker reached in a hole to see how deep it was, three young birds nibbled his fingers.

Northern flicker

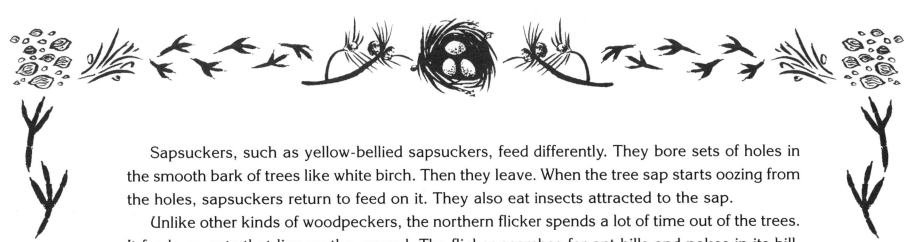

Sapsuckers, such as yellow-bellied sapsuckers, feed differently. They bore sets of holes in the smooth bark of trees like white birch. Then they leave. When the tree sap starts oozing from the holes, sapsuckers return to feed on it. They also eat insects attracted to the sap.

Unlike other kinds of woodpeckers, the northern flicker spends a lot of time out of the trees. It feeds on ants that live on the ground. The flicker searches for ant hills and pokes in its bill. Then it nabs the ants that run out or uses its sticky tongue to sweep eggs and young ants from the hill.

Homey Holes

A home for a pair of woodpeckers may take several days to make—even when both male and female work on it. The woodpeckers peck furiously, sometimes removing chunks of wood as big as your fist.

Canada's most common woodpeckers, the downy woodpeckers, take their time finding just the right tree. They seem to prefer dead trees or trees already full of holes. Often they start

Who's Holed up Now?

Woodpeckers usually peck out new homes each year, and they drill a lot of holes to find food. But as the woodpeckers move on, all these holes don't go to waste. In fact, they provide shelter for many other kinds of animals.

Some of the smallest holes become homes for mice and little birds, such as chickadees and tree swallows. To escape the heat of summer, small frogs and lizards use shady tree holes.

Larger woodpecker holes become homes for squirrels and birds, such as bluebirds and many kinds of owls, that need roomier places. If the holes are near water, ducks, such as wood ducks, mergansers and golden-eyes, may nest in them.

As trees age and rot, woodpecker holes often grow bigger, housing even larger animals. A family of big owls, opossums—even raccoons—may take over an empty woodpecker home.

Downy woodpecker

making holes in several trees before they choose the one they really want. Then they spend up to three weeks pecking out their home. The male does most of the work, drilling for about 20 minutes between breaks.

When the home is ready, the female lays four or five white eggs. Both parents take turns keeping them warm. Later, they both care for the newly hatched woodpeckers.

When the young are just 18 days old, they are almost fully grown. They crawl up the walls inside their home and poke their heads out of the hole. They often get so hungry that the parents deliver large meals to each of them about every 15 minutes.

* * *

A woodpecker's *rat-a-tat-tat* may be unwelcome noise to people who put up wooden poles for power lines. But most people welcome the sound of Canada's distant drummers. Woodpeckers eat so many wood-boring insects that they save the lives of countless trees. And the holes they drill help many other animals survive.

American White Pelicans
Super Scoopers

In the sky, big American white pelicans move with the grace and ease of a dance team. They fly in a line or vee, beating their wings slowly and deeply, keeping time with the rest of the flock. They often flap and glide great distances, unruffled even by powerful winds that cross their path.

But on land, pelicans look anything but graceful. They waddle about on short legs and red-orange, webbed feet. They have long, skinny necks and pointed, orange bills that grow up to 36 centimetres long. Beneath these bills, baggy skin stretches to form big pouches, which the birds use to scoop up water and fish.

As their name suggests, American white pelicans are mostly white. But their huge wings, which span up to three metres, are tipped with black. They are one of seven kinds of pelicans around the world. In Canada, they nest in British Columbia, Alberta, Saskatchewan, Manitoba and Ontario, spending winters along the sea coasts of southern United States and Central America.

Gone Fishing

American white pelicans eat some salamanders and frogs and a whole lot of fish. Sometimes they hunt for food alone but usually they work with other pelicans. They are one of the few kinds of animals that hunt in a group.

As they fly, pelicans use their keen eyesight to spot a school of fish. Then they land on the water and form a line, an arc or a vee. They swim with their bills open and underwater. As they near some fish, they dunk their heads—sometimes their whole necks—and use their pouches to scoop up water and fish. The clawlike tip of their bills helps grab slippery fish.

Facing a lineup of pelicans, fish try frantically to escape. They dash away from one bird's scoop but often head straight into another bird's scoop. For the pelicans, that's the beauty of fishing together.

Sometimes the birds race toward shore, flapping their wings and splashing the water. That drives the fish to the shallows where hunting is easier, and the birds feed fast and furiously.

When the pelicans lift their bills, they squeeze their pouches and drain out the water. If they've caught some fish, they point their bills upward and squeeze their pouches again and again, pushing the fish right down their throats.

It's in the Bag!

In centuries past, people believed the pouch of the pelican could stretch to huge sizes. One man said he found a human baby inside a pouch. Another claimed he had removed a soldier's hat, coat and three pairs of shoes—all from one pelican pouch. No wonder greedy people were once compared to pelicans.

Still, the pouch of the American white pelican is an amazing bag of skin. It's attached to the lower part of its bill, which can bow out like a hoop, shaping the top of the pouch. From there, the skin stretches down about 15 centimetres. It can hold as much water as an average bathroom sink—more than 11 litres—plus a fish or two. However, the pouch is not strong enough to carry the weight of water or fish. That's why pelicans drain their pouches and swallow their catches on the spot.

Minding the Nest

Not only do American white pelicans fly and fish together, they nest together. As many as several hundred gather at one spot, usually on an island in a lake where they feel safe.

Both sexes "dress up" for courting. They grow yellowish feathers across their chests and wings and a yellowish clump of feathers on their heads. Along the top of their bills, they develop a thin wafer, roughly shaped like a triangle. It drops off after the pelicans' eggs hatch.

Pelicans make a simple, shallow nest on the ground. They often build it sitting down, using their long bills to drag soil and plant material around themselves.

The female lays her eggs—usually two—and then both parents take turns looking after them. The birds keep them warm by placing one egg under each of their webbed feet. Sometimes an egg rolls out of the nest and a nearby pelican picks it up. But no pelican has three feet, so it can't care for three eggs at a time.

After a month, the first egg laid begins to hatch. Then the parents move both eggs to the tops of their feet. Two to three days later, the second egg begins to hatch.

Chicks are born weak and bare of feathers. They snuggle under their parents' wings to keep safe and warm. Pelicans feed their young thin, souplike vomit. The parents drip the vomit right into the bills of the chicks.

When the chicks are about 10 days old, they can sit up. Then they stick their bills right into the pouches of their parents to feed. The stronger they become, the more eagerly

The Egg Is Calling

When the first egg in an American white pelican nest starts to hatch, the parents give it so much attention they often forget their second egg. So it's lucky that a pelican chick can "talk" before it hatches.

Whenever it gets too hot or cold, the tiny chick cheeps—from within the egg. But it only makes one kind of sound, so the parents must decide what it needs. They either nestle down to warm the egg or stand over it to give the egg shade. The chick keeps right on cheeping until the parent bird gets it right.

they feed. Some mealtimes look like wrestling matches between a chick and its parent. One or both of them may fall over.

At three weeks, chicks gather in large, fluffy flocks that wander about while the adult birds hunt for food. But parents can easily pick their chicks out of the flocks. They keep feeding their young until the chicks are two to three months old—able to fly and find their own food.

Feeling Good

Like people, birds spend a lot of time making themselves comfortable and keeping themselves healthy. The pelican is no exception. It yawns—a comforting activity—with its neck curved beneath its bill. When it opens its bill wide, the curve of the neck presses against the bill's pouch and—just for a second—pushes it inside out. Quite a yawn!

Here are some other activities that keep an American white pelican busy when it's not fishing, flying or looking after chicks.

- Sleeping—standing up or lying on its belly
- Scratching its head and neck with a claw on its middle toe
- Nibbling and biting to clean its feathers
- Wing-shaking to rearrange its wing feathers

All Alone but Doing Fine

The American white pelicans of British Columbia seem to like nesting a long distance from other pelican colonies. Every year they fly from as far away as Mexico to Stum Lake in the middle of the province. There they make their nests on two rocky little islands, flying to other lakes to feed.

The province has tried to protect its only pelican colony by creating White Pelican Provincial Park around it. The province discourages people from using high-powered boats and low-flying planes that might disturb the nesting birds.

The colony of pelicans is doing so well that it is almost too big for Stum Lake. Biologists hope some of the pelicans will branch off one day and form a second colony in British Columbia.

- Tail-wagging to straighten its tail feathers
- Wing-flapping to stretch its wings
- Wing-thrashing and head-and-neck-dipping in water to bathe
- Leg-stretching

*　　*　　*

Good news! The number of American white pelicans across the country is rising. As Canada started protecting nesting areas and stopped using pesticides that harmed pelican eggs, these super scoopers began to thrive. Watch for them making a big vee—for victory?—in the sky as they fly.

European Starlings
Adaptable Aliens

American manufacturer Eugene Schieffelin had an odd hobby. He wanted to import every bird mentioned in the writings of British author William Shakespeare. In 1890, Mr. Schieffelin brought in 60 European starlings by boat and set them free in New York City's Central Park. And just to make sure enough survived, he imported 40 more from Europe the next year.

Not only did the starlings survive, they thrived. Every year, almost every pair raised at least two families of four or five young birds each. Soon there were too many birds for Central Park, and some starlings moved on to new homes. Today, millions of starlings—all descended from those original 100 birds—live throughout North America.

European starlings nest in countries right around the world; in Canada, they nest coast to coast. About the size of robins, they change colour through the year. From midwinter to early summer, they have yellow bills and black-feathered bodies that shine in shades of purple and green. The rest of the year, their bills appear dusky and their feathers are tipped with white spots shaped like stars. Starlings were named for these "stars," which break off as the birds go in and out of their nests.

Making Do

The European starling adapts easily to new places. That's partly because it eats several kinds of food, including human garbage and little animals, such as worms, frogs and lizards. It also eats many types of plants, grinding them in its stomach with the small stones and snail shells it swallows. But mostly, the starling eats insects. A starling family can gobble thousands a week.

Pest Arrest

The European starling doesn't like pests any more than you do. It works hard to keep itself and its nest free of creatures, such as lice, fleas, ticks and mites. It cleans its feathers by bathing, even in cold weather. Sometimes it breaks through thin ice with its sharp bill to get to water. If that's not possible, the adaptable starling spreads out its wing and tail feathers and "bathes" in the snow—or even in the smoke that rises from chimneys.

Often the starling searches out strong-smelling plants and stuffs them into its nest to turn away pests. That seems to help, but some years the pests win the battle.

Dashing across short grass, the starling feeds by stabbing the ground with the sharp point of its bill. While the bill is in the ground, the bird forces it open to make a tunnel-like hole. Then it peeks down the tunnel and looks for food, such as caterpillars and grubs.

The starling also grabs insects struck by road traffic, shakes them out of old squirrel nests, plucks them from cracks in tree bark, chases them as they fly and snatches them from other birds. And it uses much larger animals,

such as sheep and deer, for help in hunting insects. As these animals walk, they stir up insects on the ground, and they attract flying insects that the starling can nab. The bird also feeds on ticks, tiny creatures that live and feed on sheep, deer and other animals.

The starling is no fussier about its nest than it is about its food. It seems to prefer old woodpecker holes, but it moves into almost any kind of shelter. It nests inside junk cars and airplanes and behind broken window panes in garages. Sometimes it tries to nest in the engines and wings of airplanes still in use, so workers check the planes and remove any nesting material.

Hanging Out

At night, European starlings like to gang together in huge numbers. That way they stay warmer and safer. A few hours before sunset, they start gathering high up in trees or on buildings. From there, they fly up, down and around as one thick mass and head to their main roost, or resting place. In summer, it might be a grove of leaf-covered trees; in winter, a big building or a

Bird Buddy

In the 1700s, a starling, named Starl, lived with one of the world's most famous music composers—Wolfgang Amadeus Mozart of Austria. The bird was Mozart's buddy. The two of them spent a lot of time together, even when Mozart was working. One day, Starl thrilled its master by whistling a line of Mozart's own music. Like all starlings, it was good at imitating sounds.

The day Starl died, Mozart wrote a poem to honour the bird he loved so much. He also held a big funeral in his garden. Soon after, he produced a strange piece of music, full of clumsy rhythms and notes that didn't seem to fit. Even the ending was very odd and very sudden. Called *The Musical Joke,* it puzzled music experts for years. Now they think that Starl may have inspired Mozart to write it. Perhaps the composer was imitating the many sounds his starling made.

bridge. Starlings often use the same roost over a long time. In Europe, they have used some roosts for more than 150 years.

When the flock reaches its roost, the birds swarm above it, then dive straight down. As they take their places on the roost, they number from several hundred to a quarter of a million—sometimes more. When young starlings join them late in summer, the flocks are especially large. In cities where masses have roosted on the huge hands of town clocks, the birds have even managed to "stop time" in its track.

Gathered together, European starlings make a terrific racket. Large flocks are heard far away from their roosts. But by morning, they take off in much smaller groups. They may gather again for a short while in the afternoon, and then go their own ways until it's time to head for the roost.

The Barber's Starling

A village barber had a starling that learned to talk. It imitated its master, saying such things as "I am the master barber," "Well, well, did you ever!" and "I like company." People stopped by the barber shop just to hear the starling speak. They laughed when the words it said seemed to suit what they were talking about.

One day, the starling escaped through an open window and joined some other birds. After feeding, they all flew off together—and headed straight into a trap. Most of the birds whistled and hissed, but the barber's starling said, "Well, well, did you ever!"

When the bird-catcher came, he began removing the birds, one by one. But when he came to the barber's starling, the bird looked him in the eye and said, "I am the master barber."

The bird-catcher was startled . . . then afraid . . . then amused. A laugh rolled right up from his belly and he said, "You must be the barber's bird. How did you get into my trap?"

"I like company," said the starling. "I like company."

—*an old story from Germany*

Sounding Off

Few birds make as many sounds as the European starling. When it sings, it produces a soft, fast set of notes that it repeats and repeats. But it also makes a wide range of weird and wonderful noises: whistling, clicking, squeaking, bubbling, chortling, coughing and sneezing.

In some countries, such as China, people value the starling because it is a great imitator. It can make many of the sounds that it hears, including the calls of other birds. In fact, the starling can imitate about 30 different kinds of birds, such as blue jays, bobwhites, robins and crows.

The starling also imitates other kinds of animals, barking like dogs, meowing like cats, croaking like frogs—even talking like people. Imitating things that are big and loud helps the starling frighten away its enemies. Probably the loudest noises it makes sound just like burglar alarms and telephones.

*   *   *

European starlings are not popular birds. Their huge, noisy flocks take over parks and buildings in cities and towns. But, although they were once aliens, they've adapted extremely well to life in Canada. So we'd better get used to the fact—even enjoy it: starlings are here to stay.

Mute swan

Swans

Feathered Grace

For centuries, poets and novelists have written about the charm and grace of the swan. They have described its wings as "folded glory" and its feathers as "white perfection." Artists have preserved its beauty in paintings and in carvings of gold and silver.

Five kinds of swans live around the world; three in Canada. Whistling swans—also called tundra swans—nest in northern parts of Manitoba, Ontario, Quebec and the Yukon and Northwest territories. Trumpeter swans breed in British Columbia, Alberta, Saskatchewan and the Yukon and Northwest territories. And mute swans, once brought as captive birds from Europe, now live wild in parts of British Columbia, Saskatchewan and Ontario. They stay year round, but whistling and some trumpeter swans fly to the United States each fall.

All of Canada's swans are white with black feet. Whistling and trumpeter swans have black bills, but the mute swan has an orange bill with a black knob at its base.

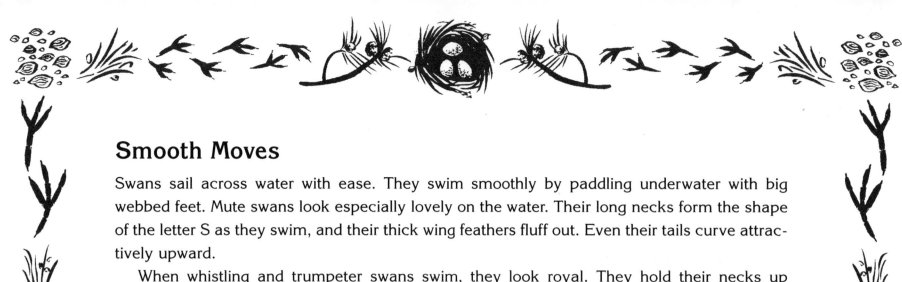

Smooth Moves

Swans sail across water with ease. They swim smoothly by paddling underwater with big webbed feet. Mute swans look especially lovely on the water. Their long necks form the shape of the letter S as they swim, and their thick wing feathers fluff out. Even their tails curve attractively upward.

When whistling and trumpeter swans swim, they look royal. They hold their necks up straight and their wings close to their bodies. The only time their necks are curved is when the birds feed or get upset.

None of the swans dive, but sometimes they poke their bills into water so deep their tails point straight up. That happens during feedings. The birds eat water plants and may need to reach far down to grab them.

When swans take off from the water, they use a long runway. Thrashing their wings and slapping their feet, they look as if they are racing across the water. When they are airborne, they fly with their necks flat out and their feet trailing behind them. Once more, they are a vision of grace.

Moving their wings in deep, slow beats, swans can fly as fast as cars travel on a high-

---

Snakelike Swan

The long neck of a swan is so flowing it seems snakelike. That's not surprising. It's made of more sections of bone, called vertebrae, than the neck of any other bird, or any mammal. The mute swan, for instance, has twenty-five vertebrae in its neck, while the giraffe has only seven.

But the swan's neck is not all that reminds us of snakes. Like every kind of bird, swans evolved—over millions of years—from reptiles. And they still share some traits with these relatives: the eggs they lay to produce their young, the shape of the bone around their eyes, and the scales that cover their legs and feet. But over time, the scales that once covered their entire bodies gradually became long and flat, forming the feathers that swans and other birds wear today.

Trumpeter swan

way. And when trumpeter and whistling swans migrate, they fly even faster. Then masses of birds form a long line or a big vee across the sky. They sail along 10 to 100 metres above the ground, often rising to 1500—sometimes 3000—metres on long trips. When they descend, they swoop across the water and come to a smooth stop—without a splash.

Wild Calls

Swans make calls but little music—although their beating wings hum like vibrating strings. In fact, the wings of mute swans make much more sound than their calls. Angry or frightened mute swans just hiss or snort. Friendly mute swans make a soft "chirring" sound. The mothers sometimes yap like puppies to their young. But most of the time, these swans say nothing at all.

Although you might expect whistling swans to whistle, they don't. They make high-pitched "wow-how-oo" calls instead, so no one knows for sure how they got their name. On the water, they are often silent. Sometimes they murmur, cluck or "laugh" softly. Other times, they call out loudly. But whistling swans make the most noise when they fly, forming a big chorus in the sky.

Low-pitched "ko-huh" sounds come from the trumpeter swan. It calls through an extra long windpipe that loops up and over a hump of bone, producing a loud, trumpetlike sound. Like whistling swans, trumpeters are usually quiet on the water and noisy in the air. Flocks trumpet so loudly they can be heard more than three kilometres away. That helps the swans keep together during long flights.

Wonder Swans

Canada's swans are not only beautiful, they're remarkable birds. Some of these facts may surprise you.

Swan in Ballet Shoes

The graceful movements of swans inspired world-famous ballerina Anna Pavlova. All her life, she loved nature. Ever since she began dancing as a child in Russia in 1891, much of her ballet was about nature, including snowflakes, butterflies and poppies. But the dance her audiences loved most was about swans.

When Anna danced *The Dying Swan,* her feet moved so smoothly she glided—as though floating across still water. She moved her wrists and arms softly, gently, like the wings of a swan. And her entire body quivered and fluttered like a dying bird.

Anna loved the mute swans that lived on a lake by her house. She attracted them with a warm laugh and a soft call. "Come here, come on," she would say—and they would. Swans were part of her life right to the end. As she was dying, she whispered to her maid, "Get my swan costume ready."

- The wings of trumpeter swans span nearly 2.5 metres. Trumpeters are the biggest swans on Earth.
- Mute swans are one of the heaviest birds that fly. They can weigh 18 to 20 kilograms. One weighed 22.5 kilograms—but it was too heavy to fly.
- The feathers on one whistling swan totalled 25 216. Swans grow very dense coats of feathers and down, which help keep them warm and afloat in water.
- Trumpeter swans sometimes nest on top of empty muskrat houses.
- Usually only one pair of swans nests in a lake—even if the lake is large.
- When swans break out of their eggshells, their eyes are already open and their bodies are clothed with soft, fluffy feathers. What's more, they're ready to run.

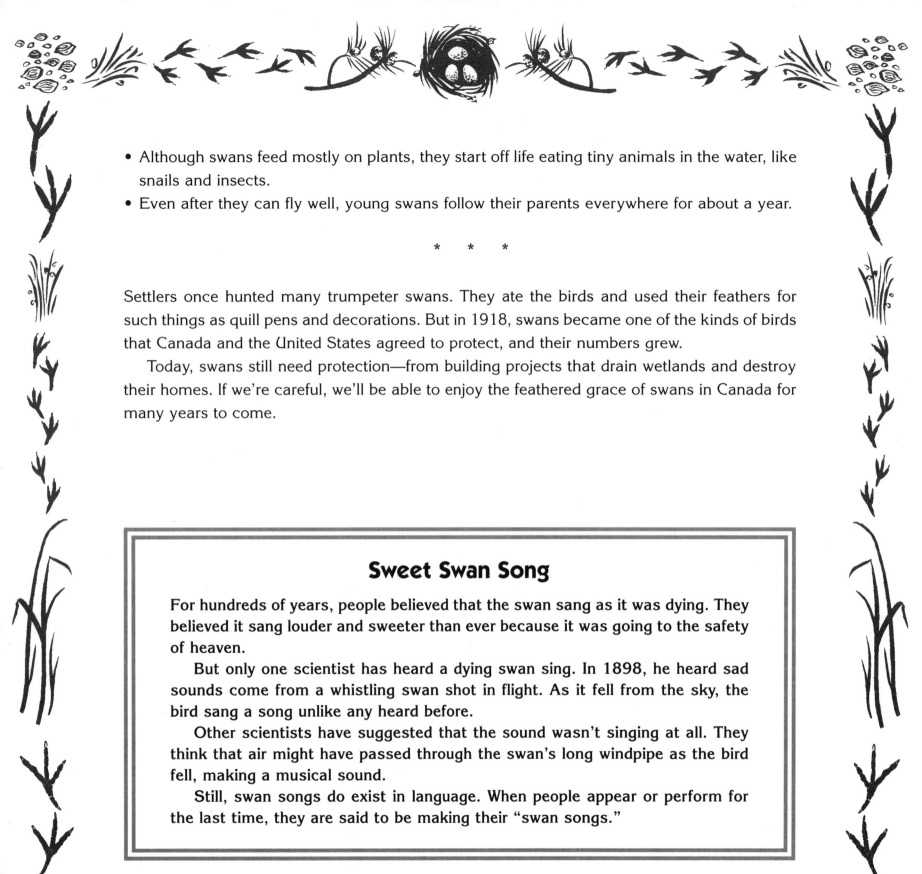

- Although swans feed mostly on plants, they start off life eating tiny animals in the water, like snails and insects.
- Even after they can fly well, young swans follow their parents everywhere for about a year.

*   *   *

Settlers once hunted many trumpeter swans. They ate the birds and used their feathers for such things as quill pens and decorations. But in 1918, swans became one of the kinds of birds that Canada and the United States agreed to protect, and their numbers grew.

Today, swans still need protection—from building projects that drain wetlands and destroy their homes. If we're careful, we'll be able to enjoy the feathered grace of swans in Canada for many years to come.

Sweet Swan Song

For hundreds of years, people believed that the swan sang as it was dying. They believed it sang louder and sweeter than ever because it was going to the safety of heaven.

But only one scientist has heard a dying swan sing. In 1898, he heard sad sounds come from a whistling swan shot in flight. As it fell from the sky, the bird sang a song unlike any heard before.

Other scientists have suggested that the sound wasn't singing at all. They think that air might have passed through the swan's long windpipe as the bird fell, making a musical sound.

Still, swan songs do exist in language. When people appear or perform for the last time, they are said to be making their "swan songs."

Acknowledgements

I am sincerely grateful to the experts who so carefully reviewed the chapters in this book: Dave Fraser of Arenaria Research and Interpretation; Myke Chutter and Syd Cannings of the British Columbia Ministry of Environment, Lands and Parks; Steve Johnson of L.G.L. Ltd.; Dick Cannings and Lee Gass of the University of British Columbia; and Ken Morgan and Rick McKelvey of the Canadian Wildlife Service.

Thanks also to Doug Penhale for his fantastic bird art and to my hubby, Wayne, who always cheers me on when the going gets tough.

Index

About the Author

Diane Swanson lives on Vancouver Island, B.C. Her articles on nature and wildlife have appeared in children's magazines *Ranger Rick* and *Owl*. She is the author of five "Our Choice" children's books: *A Toothy Tongue and One Long Foot, Why Seals Blow Their Noses, Squirts and Snails and Skinny Green Tails, Safari Beneath the Sea* and *Coyotes in the Crosswalk*. Diane Swanson is also the author of *The Emerald Sea*.

About the Illustrator

Douglas Penhale is a freelance artist living on Saltspring Island, B.C. His avid interest in nature, together with a move to the west coast, turned him from commercial art to wildlife illustration. His nature drawings and cartoons have been featured in many books and magazines, and he was the Grand Prize Winner at the International Cartoon Festival in 1985. Douglas Penhale has also illustrated *Coyotes in the Crosswalk, Why Seals Blow Their Noses,* and *The Coastal Birder's Journal*.